big

D1079451

90710 000 475 051

For Yil, Kurt and Derya—thank you for always encouraging me to dream big—S.A.

OXFORD
UNIVERSITY PRESS

Great Clarendon Street, Oxford OX2 6DP

Oxford University Press is a department of the University of Oxford.
It furthers the University's objective of excellence in research, scholarship,
and education by publishing worldwide. Oxford is a registered trade mark of
Oxford University Press in the UK and in certain other countries

Text and illustrations © Sav Akyüz 2021

The moral rights of the author and artist have been asserted

Database right Oxford University Press (maker)

First published 2021

All rights reserved. No part of this publication may be reproduced,
stored in a retrieval system, or transmitted, in any form or by any means,
without the prior permission in writing of Oxford University Press,
or as expressly permitted by law, or under terms agreed with the appropriate
reprographics rights organization. Enquiries concerning reproduction
outside the scope of the above should be sent to the Rights Department,
Oxford University Press, at the address above.

You must not circulate this book in any other binding or cover
and you must impose this same condition on any acquirer

British Library Cataloguing in Publication Data available

ISBN: 978-0-19-277955-7 (paperback)

1 3 5 7 9 10 8 6 4 2

Printed in China

Paper used in the production of this book is a natural, recyclable product made
from wood grown in sustainable forests. The manufacturing process conforms
to the environmental regulations of the country of origin

DISCARDED

LONDON BOROUGH OF RICHMOND UPON THAMES	
90710 000 475 051	
Askews & Holts	04-Jun-2021
JF	
RTCA	

big

SAV AKYÜZ

OXFORD

UNIVERSITY PRESS

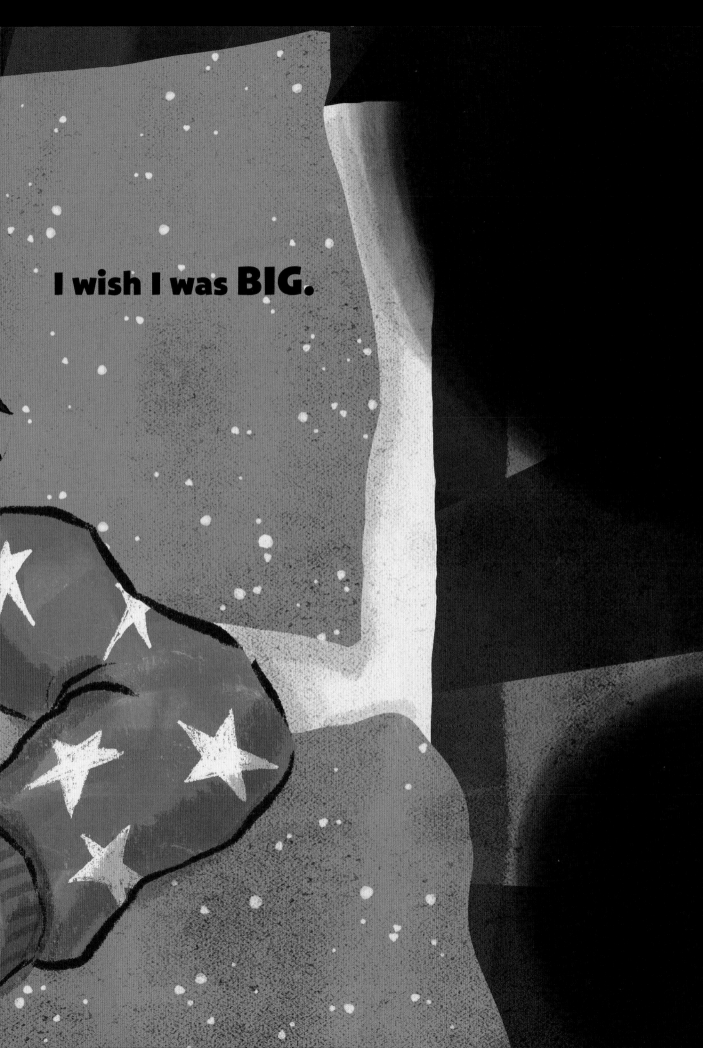

I wish I was BIG.

I LOVE being BIG!

I'm TOO big!

I like being small.

**For now
I'll just
dream big.**